I Wish I Could of Said

"Goodbye"

KELLY HUSTON FLAHERTY

WestBow Press books may be ordered through booksellers or by contacting:

WestBow Press
A Division of Thomas Nelson & Zondervan
1663 Liberty Drive
Bloomington, IN 47403
www.westbowpress.com
1 (866) 928-1240

ISBN: 978-1-5127-3550-5 (sc)
ISBN: 978-1-5127-3551-2 (e)

Library of Congress Control Number: 2016904599

Print information available on the last page.

WestBow Press rev. date: 4/21/2016

WESTBOW
P R E S S®
A DIVISION OF THOMAS NELSON
& ZONDERVAN

In the communion of *saints we believe that our
relationships are stronger than death
- Cardinal Francis George

* For the sake of children angels are being portrayed

Tommy came home from school with a sad look on his face.

"What is it Tommy?" Mom asked in a hurry, "why do you look so worried?"

"It is my friend Dean, he is no longer here.
Our teacher told us while shedding a tear."

"She said he has died he has gone up above.
She said he's with God surrounded by love."

"She means he's in heaven." mom said with some cheer,
"Can you feel him above he is very near?"

"What do you mean?"
Tommy asked with his eyes full of gleam.

Mom replied with gentle care,
"Dean is still here,
he is everywhere."

"How do you know he is everywhere?"
Tommy said with a little pout.

"You must believe my sweet dear
and not have any doubt."

"Do you believe in angels?"
Mom said with joy.

"ANGELS!" Tommy shouted,
"Please tell me more."

"They are here my love holding us tight.
They are here sweet boy no need for fright."

Tommy replied, "I don't understand,
are the angels around us here on land?"
He leaned in closer and whispered out loud,
"can we see the angels here on the ground?"

"We can't see the angels with our eyes
we rely on our faith when someone dies."

"Can you talk to them without seeing their face?'

Mom hugged Tommy and answered with grace,
"They love so much when you talk to them,
tell them your dreams,
your hopes or your fears.
They will help guide you and calm your heart my dear."

"They will hear you and they will come.
Open your heart and let them in.
Sit still my love," mom said with a grin.

"I think angels are here all around,
they are waiting patiently for you to stop and be still.
They want to be found."

"I think I get it" Tommy said with joy.

"Think of it this way my sweet little boy."………

"The sparkle of water on a still lake."

"The awe of a mountain and a beautiful landscape."

"The delicate shape of
an intricate snowflake."

"The song of a bird on a
crisp sunny day."

"These my sweet child are a few of the ways
angels show their love to us everyday."

"I miss him already," Tommy started to cry,
"I wish I could of said good-bye."

Tommy was stricken with a sense of peace,
"Oh mom" he said, "its good to know Dean is always here with me."

"Tommy" mom said, "one last advice,
aren't you so glad you were always so nice?"

In memory of Quinn Kirsch
and for all those who never got to say goodbye

CPSIA information can be obtained
at www.ICGtesting.com
Printed in the USA
BVOW07s1924230516

449232BV00001B/1/P